THE LEMON DROP JAR

THE
LEMON DROP JAR

by Christine Widman
illustrated by Christa Kieffer

Simon & Schuster Books for Young Readers

SIMON & SCHUSTER BOOKS FOR YOUNG READERS
An imprint of Simon & Schuster Children's Publishing Division
1230 Avenue of the Americas
New York, New York 10020

The text of this book is set in 16 pt. Goudy Old Style.
The illustrations are rendered in watercolor.

First Edition
Printed in Hong Kong
10 9 8 7 6 5 4

Library of Congress Cataloging-in-Publication Data
Widman, Christine Barker.
The lemon drop jar / by Christine Widman ; illustrated by Christa
Kieffer. — 1st ed.
p.   cm.
Summary: A little girl makes a winter visit to her great-aunt, who
brings out her lemon drop jar to brighten the gray day, stimulating
family memories.
ISBN 0-02-792759-8
[1. Great-aunts—Fiction.]   I. Kieffer, Christa, ill.   II. Title.
PZ7.W6346Le   1992   [E]—dc20   91-11209

To Tuppie—C.W.

For Ella—C. K.

I'm staying with my great-aunt Emma. I came on a train all by myself. Aunt Emma met me at the station. She gave me a small paper bag, filled with lemon drops. Aunt Emma always knows what I like.

Her house is full of treasures. Today she took
a glass jar out of her big china cupboard and put
it on the window ledge in the kitchen.

"What's that?" I ask.

"It's my lemon drop jar," she says. "On gray days like today, we need the lemon drops to invite the sun in."

Aunt Emma and I fill the jar with lemon drops and then we take a walk.

I wear my woolly hat and mittens. The wind is rough. It pushes me. Out in the woods the yellow leaves drop, drop, drop from the trees. Aunt Emma and I toss leaves in the air. Yellow is everywhere. "It's like being inside the lemon drop jar," I say.

We come back to the house early. Aunt Emma puts her hands on my cheeks and we touch noses.

"My, my," she says, "your nose is cold. Time for lemon tea."

"I've never had lemon tea before," I say.

"That's because you've only been here in the summer. I make lemon tea when winter is coming," says Aunt Emma.

She lights a log in the fireplace. Her yellow cat runs over and curls up beside me. I watch the fingers of fire grow tall and twisty. The log cracks and pops.

Aunt Emma brings our tea in cups with tiny yellow roses on them. She brings the lemon drop jar, too. She stirs a lemon drop into each cup.

"Why did you do that?" I ask.

"To make our tea sweet and tangy," she says.

I touch the lemon drop jar. Part of it is smooth and clear and part of it is rough, where flowers and feathers are cut into the glass.

"Where did you get the lemon drop jar?" I ask.

"When I was a little girl," says Aunt Emma, "I lived where it was always warm, and the sun was always bright yellow in the sky. We had a lemon tree in our backyard. Your great-granmama and I made our own lemon drops from the lemons on our tree.

"When I got bigger, I went away to school on a train. I cried when I waved good-bye to Mama and Papa."

"I cry when I say good-bye to you."

"I know," says Aunt Emma.

She gives me a lemon drop. She takes one, too.

"Then what happened?" I ask.

"At school," says Aunt Emma, "winter came.

"I wrote to Mama, It's cold here. I miss the sun.

"I wrote to Papa, It's snowing and snowing. Is the yellow sun shining for you and Mama today?

"Your great-granmama knew I was homesick. She knew I missed the sun. She knew I missed the lemon tree in our backyard.

"One snowy winter day a package arrived. *For Emma*, it said."

"What was it?" I ask.

"Everyone in school asked that, too. They crowded around me. I opened the package. Inside was the crystal jar you're holding now, filled with lemon drops. I knew Mama had sent a hundred little suns, just for me."

"Will I see the lemon drop jar when I come next summer?" I ask.

"No," says Aunt Emma, "I only bring it out in winter, when I get homesick for the sun. It reminds me of Mama...and now it will remind me of you."

We sip our tea.

The cat purrs a soft song.

The wind blows the sun off the edge of the earth.

"Goodness me," says Aunt Emma. "It's time for supper."

She lights a lamp. Its yellow glow spreads
across the braided rug and the sleeping cat.

I carry the lemon drop jar into the kitchen
and put it on the ledge.

Frost has made feathers on the window. I
trace them with my finger.

A yellow moon shines in the dark sky.

I watch the lemon drop moon through the
lemon drop jar window.

Someday, I'm going to have a lemon drop jar,
but I won't put it away. I'll keep it by my
window all the time...to remind me of Aunt
Emma.